Rocky the Cockatoo

By: Heather Lee Beyer

To order additional copies of this book, contact:
Xlibris
844-714-8691
www.Xlibris.com
Orders@Xlibris.com

ISBN: 978-1-6641-6405-5 (sc)
ISBN: 978-1-6641-6406-2 (e)

Print information available on the last page

Rev. date: 03/11/2024

This story takes place in an avian nature setting

The main character of the story is a young parakeet, named Rocky

Rocky is going through identity emotions; she is a parakeet that wants to be a cockatoo

Her classmates and friends don't understand the way she feels and laugh at her.

Rocky's mother tries to cheer her up when she arrives home from School and as they talk and laugh, Time goes by very fast

Rocky's mom soon forgets the time for dinner and sends Rocky outside to get her brother.

Rocky's brother is in trouble when his foot is stuck under the branches and Rocky becomes the heroine of the story.

By the end of the story, Rocky with the help of her mother's advice: learns to accept who she is.

This is a simple story for young kids, for they are so impressionable.

ROCKY THE "COCKATOO"

In a small town, in a tall bush lived a young parakeet named Rocky. Rocky had a long blue tail, white feathers and black spots on her wings. She was a beautiful parakeet, but that wasn't good enough for her. Rocky wanted to be a cockatoo.

Rocky shared her home with her Mom, Dad and her little brother Blue. One night Rocky's mother screeched "Rocky, clean your nest, and pick up your seed!"

"But Mom I don't want to" Rocky yelled back at her mom. "You'll know, if I was a cockatoo. I wouldn't have to clean up my room"

Rocky's mom sighed and she replied, "How do you know that? Every bird has to clean their nest."

Rocky said in a hurry, "Cockatoos are big! They do what they want!"

"But Rocky, honey", her mother said sadly. "if you were a cockatoo, you wouldn't be my daughter. You'd belong to some other family and I would never know you. That would make me very sad."

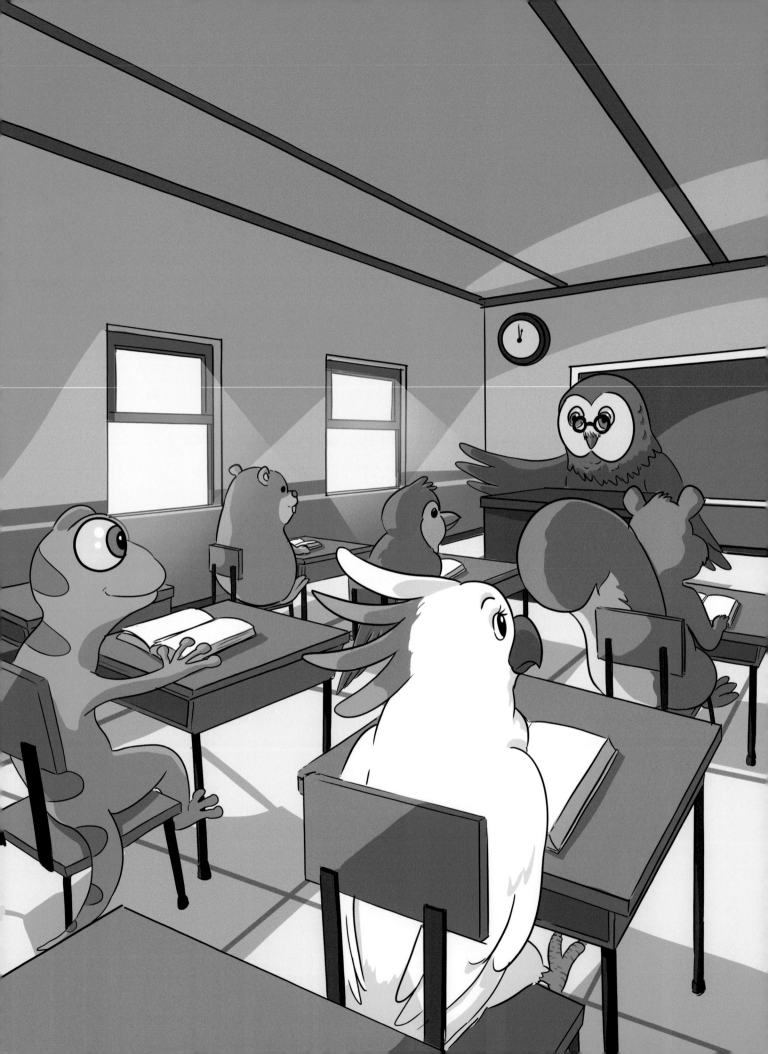

Every morning before school, Rocky would clean her beak and wings. She would use her beak to clean all her feathers. She would admire herself in the mirror. She loved the blue color on her tail and belly. She liked the way her feathers stood up when she chirped. It wasn't enough though, she wanted to be like the other girl cockatoos in school. Rocky said to herself, "I wish I were a cockatoo".

While at school one morning, Rocky's teacher, Miss Sims asked the class to write a paragraph about

"What I want to be when I grow up." She gave the class a few minutes to write their thoughts on paper.

"Okay Class", Miss Sims announced. "Pencils down". After lunch we will read our paragraphs out loud."

Rocky could hardly wait to read hers.

After lunch, one by one, all the students read their paragraphs. Some wanted to fight nest fires, one wanted to fix broken wings, and others wanted to clean nests. It was now Rocky's turn. She puffed out her chest and read, "I want to be a cockatoo" "A cockatoo is big. A cockatoo is proud" Rocky continued "Cockatoos Bob their heads up and flap their wings." "A cockatoo squawks and squeals and they get everyone's attention." All the other kids laughed at her, because Rocky was a parakeet, not a cockatoo.

That afternoon, Rocky walked home sad. She was upset, because the other birds didn't understand her. She knew one person would, her mom. When Rocky walked through the door. She shouted, "Mom, where are you? I want to read something to you"

"I'm in the kitchen, Rocky. Come in here", Rocky's mom yelled back

Rocky read her paper to mom with a proud voice

Mom smiled

Mom was sad for Rocky that the other kids laughed so she told her silly things she did when she was a young parakeet. She told Rocky jokes to make her laugh and the afternoon went by very fast

"Rocky", her mother said. "Can you go get your brother from the yard outside and tell him dinner is ready."

"Okay, mom" said Rocky

Rocky went out into the yard and called her brother, "Brother, where are you?" "Mom says to come back to the nest for dinner" There was no answer. But then suddenly, Rocky heard her brother, "Help! Help me!" he cried. Rocky rushed to her brother's side.

"Help Rocky, my foot is stuck"

She carefully walked around the bush and saw that his foot was twisted underneath a large branch. "Don't cry, I'll get you free!" Rocky's brother, Blue was scared. That branch was heavy and he was little. Rocky pushed her beak underneath the branch, but it wouldn't budge. Then she tried again, it wouldn't move. Blue started to cry. Finally, Rocky tried to move the branch to the other side and because her beak was small and thin, she was able to fit underneath the branch and she freed Blue's foot at last.

"Everything is going to be alright now, Blue!", said Rocky "You saved me!", exclaimed a delighted Blue "Come on, let's go home.", said Rocky Rocky and her brother flew back home to the nest as fast as they could

"Mom, Dad. Rocky saved me! I was playing in the yard and the tree branch fell on my leg. I was there for a long time, yelling but no one heard me. I was so scared. But then Rocky came. She lifted the heavy branch with her beak even though there was hardly any room. I lifted my foot and I was free!" he shouted. Blue spoke so fast, his parents almost missed what he said.

"Are you okay, Blue? Rocky?" Mom asked them

"Yes, Mom. Blue and I are fine., don't worry. I helped him." Rocky told her mother

Rocky's mom kissed the top of her beak. "Thanks, Rocky for saving your brother!"

"Okay Kids", Dad said. "I am going to help Mother clean the dishes. Please go upstairs and wash your beak and claws. Mom will be up to tuck you in for the night."

Rocky and her brother did what they were told and went to their rooms.

"Goodnight, Rocky", Blue said

Good night, Blue" Rocky yelled back towards Blue.

That night before going to sleep, Rocky lay awake in her bed. She took a deep breath while remembering the day's events.

"Knock, knock" Rocky's mom said while entering Rocky's room.

"Hi Mom, did you come to say good night to me?"

"Yes, but I wanted to talk to you," her mother said "Rocky, do you realize you saved your brother's life today, because you are a small parakeet and not a cockatoo? Your beak was small enough to get underneath the large branch? A cockatoo's bill would have been too big to save your brother. "Rocky thought about it. She smiled to herself.

"I guess you're right Mom. I never thought about it that way."

"I am glad, Rocky. You know sometimes we all want to be someone different.". Do you know what is special about you?"

"I can tweet for a long time. I don't make a mess of my seed and I like to help others", Rocky replied.

"You see, maybe secretly, other birds want to be brave like you", mom said as she shut off the light.

"Yes, Mom."

"Good night and sweet dreams, Rocky", mom kissed her head.

The night was quiet. Rocky settled down in her hay and branches

Rocky slowly closed her eyes and said to herself, "I'm a Parakeet."

Printed in the United States
by Baker & Taylor Publisher Services